Super team X

*Inferno Touch*

# Cyscoprime Publishers

**An Imprint of Evincepub Publishing**
Parijat Extension, Bilaspur, Chhattisgarh 495001
First Published by Cyscoprime Publishers 2020
Copyright © Huzaifa 2020
All Rights Reserved.
**ISBN:** 978-93-90047-20-8
**Price:**RS.115/-

# Super teamX

*Inferno Touch*

By

*Huzaifa*

*Dedicated to My Mom for Her Love and Support.*
*Mom, You Are My Angel.*

# Preface

My first experience of writing a book was hard enough to exhaust anybody, but yes, it was very adventurous and very exciting. Moreover, I could say it is a fusion of many emotions like excitement, anxiety, happiness, fear, nervousness, confusion, but above all, I was very positive about the stories which I had come up through. I must admit that how I got the adventurous idea of writing a book is not a very old thought; it just clicked in my mind, and moreover, the curiosity for writing came with the storybooks which I used to get from my uncle (Doctor Wajid Ali Khan) and my aunt (Subuhi Sherwani). Thank you so much for creating this passion. Since then, I was chasing this dream. It is worth to mention that it would not have been possible for me to complete this without the support of my mother and my dad for their untiring efforts, Injila, my younger sister, for being always by my side, my maternal grandparents, my uncles and aunts and my beloved cousins. Can't forget Sadiya, domestic help for giving me a cup of coffee when I was feeling exhausted. Last but not least my friend, Darsh Yadav, who has given me the ideas and supported me throughout this journey.

*Love you all*

*-Huzaifa*

# About The Book

*This book is written by Mohammad Huzaifa. This book is based on superheroes. The story revolves around Noah Marshal, the son of Emma and Lucas Marshal. He had superpowers but he didn't know it. Noah had lost his parents. Noah was supported by his brother-like friend, Zeo Rodriguez. Zeo also had powers that were hidden from them. They came to know that Noah's parents were superheroes. Noah also has to become one. Zeo helps Noah. They became superheroes. Soon, they met Jane, an A.I.*

# About the Author

*This is Mohammad Huzaifa. He studies in class 6th in DPS Noida. It is for the first time that he wrote a book. He was always inspired by Superheroes. The first book he read was "Marvel's 5-Minutes stories." His most liked superheroes are Spider-Man, Iron Man, Batman and Superman.*

# Prologue

*Once upon a time, in 1999, in California, America, there was a huge mansion in which there lived four people. A man, Lucas Marshal, his wife, Emma Marshal, their son, Noah Marshal and a baby boy Siberian husky named Ulva. Well, Noah was born in 1999. So, he is a newborn baby right now. Lucas used to work in the American army and had fought a lot for his country. That doesn't mean that he is dead. He is still alive. 10 years later, On 5 April 2009, Lucas left and promised to come on Noah's 10th birthday. After 11 days of waiting and arranging, it was 16th April, Noah's birthday. The whole mansion was decorated with lights, balloons and ribbons. The table was also a lot decorated. The time was already 8:00 pm and there was no news about Lucas. Emma called Lucas several times, but his phone was out of reach. Suddenly, the doorbell rang. Noah and Emma hoped that it should be Lucas. Emma opened the door and saw that it was Noah's pals and Stephen Hicken's, Lucas's friend in the army. They all gave Noah his gifts and sat on the couch there. Stephen rose and went to Emma and whispered "Emma, we have lost Lucas in a war against Russia. When we were entering the border of Russia, in order to finish our enemies, they threw fire out of their flamethrowers, and Lucas got hit by the fire and we lost him." Emma was crying but she didn't show it to anybody. She didn't tell anything to Noah. But secretly, Noah had eavesdropped Stephen and Emma. Now, Noah knows everything. But still he was enjoying the party with everyone. After the darkness of the night passed away and the rays of the sun fell on mansion, Noah woke and asked Emma "Mom, is father dead?" Emma said "Yes." They both cried a lot. After some time, they performed the funeral but*

*without the body. Noah was in 6th class when he lost his dad. 9 years passed away since Lucas's death, Noah had completed his college and now he is 19 years old. As he reached home, he saw a person who had covered his face with an air mask and had wrapped himself in fire. That person was burning Emma. Noah ran and got a bucket full of water and threw it at that person. That person was flying away but Noah got hold of that guy's leg and bashed him on the floor. That person was trying to fly away but Noah brought a knife and stabbed it in that person's hand. But that person kicked Noah in the jaw after which Noah was unconscious and that person flew away.*

# Contents

# <u>*Chapter 1: No! Not Again!*</u>

*After some time, Noah heard a voice that sounded a lot familiar. The voice was repeating Noah's name continuously like a thousand times. The voice was sounding in tension. Soon the voice divided into two. Soon, Noah opened his eyes and saw Zeo Rodriguez, Noah's college pal, and Mr. Walter, Noah's family doctor. Noah soon saw that he was on a stretcher. He said, as he stared Mr. Walter and Zeo in amazement "Mr. Walter, Zeo! You people here? What happened? And why am I here?" Soon, Noah gathered his memories. He asked Mr. Walter about his mother and came to know that she is very new to death. Noah asked about the room of the hospital in which Noah was admitted. Mr. Walter said "It's room no. 4207." Noah took out all the nasogastric tubes connected to his body and ran towards the room no. 4207. Zeo grabbed the injection of instant sleep and ran towards Noah. Noah soon gained success in finding his mother's room. He then rushed inside and saw his mother breathing heavily. Noah sat near his mother when suddenly, Emma grabbed Noah's hand said "Noah, Noah, please. Take care of yourself and all your friends." Noah asked in a hurry, crying "Mom, who had burnt you?" Emma says "There are 8 containers which have a liquid of different colors each. The person who burnt me is after them. The person who burnt me was the one who murdered your dad. His name is Infer...." Emma had left Noah all alone. When suddenly, Emma caught her breath for some time and passed Noah a container, saying "I had one of the containers with me till this moment. But now, promise me that you'll keep it safe whatever it takes." Noah was crying a lot but still he said, his voice trembling in sadness "Y-y-y-yes. I p-p-promi-promise." Then, Emma died. Noah suddenly felt an injection on his neck and he slept instantly. And then Zeo took out the injection, picked Noah up, went to Noah's mansion, put him to bed and put him to sleep.*

*Noah was still conscious but his body can't move. He saw someone. He soon recognized him. He was the one who was putting Emma on fire. It looked like Mr. Stephen Hickens was lying to Emma. It looked like he is the culprit in all of these incidents. It can't be a coincidence. It looked like he knew the person who had killed Emma. Suddenly, he saw something but it was hazy. Soon, it all cleared up.*

# <u>*Chapter 2: Life-Long Secret*</u>

*Noah saw Lucas and Emma. He saw a room which was hidden from him. Noah suddenly woke up and saw it was 5:00 am. He went to the washroom and took a bath. After some time, Noah came out with his pants. He soon went into the kitchen and found Zeo making pancakes for himself and Noah. Noah ran and saw the door which he saw in the dream. Noah tried a lot to open the door. But he failed. He then broke the door open and fell down the stairs which were present there. Noah was unconscious once again and was taken to the hospital of Mr. Walter. Soon it was 9:00 pm when suddenly Noah regained consciousness. He was at home. There was a bandage on his head. He had a look in the fridge and saw that there were no eggs and no milk. He took some money and left for the supermarket. In the way, some people came and tried to steal the money. Noah fought a lot against them a lot but he lost. Noah was injured a lot. Those people were going, laughing and counting the money when suddenly, Noah stood up and his eyes were pure white. He was wholly surrounded by fire. He then ran towards the people and jumped towards them. He also then fought with those people and the thieves surrendered. He then took everybody to the police station. After some time, he was back to normal but was feeling very powerless, weak and dizzy. He then went to the market, bought the eggs and milk when he remembered that Ulva has passed years ago so he went and bought two puppies Siberian husky's and returned to the mansion. Noah and Zeo ate the dinner, Zeo also gave the puppies pedigree. Then, Noah went to the room in which he fell. Suddenly, he slipped and fell head first into a slimy liquid. He then took it out and saw a huge lab. Noah then went upstairs and decided to explore that futuristic place the next morning. He went into his room and slept. Zeo slept on the couch as usual and the dogs slept in the living room. The next morning, he woke up and told Zeo about the room. Zeo said "Yeah, I think our college studied science would help us upgrade the things present there." They all went into the room and Noah said "I wish I could turn on the lights." The lights suddenly turned on when a girlish voice came out of nowhere "Turning on the lights. Welcome, Mr. Lucas and Ms. Emma." Noah said "Hey, I am Noah, the son of Lucas and Emma, and he is Zeo, my friend." The girl asked "Then, what happened to Mr. Lucas and Ms. Emma?" Noah told everything to that girl and asked "Who are you? When were you born?" The girl said "I am Jane, an A.I. I am not born, I was made in 1998, which means I was made 20 years before now." Zeo said "It looks like we're in the future's future of future." Noah said "Yeah, so futuristic technology it is?" Jane started malfunctioning a lot. Noah says "Ummmm …. No, maybe I'm wrong." She said "Sirrrrrr* computer malfunction* please you need to give the electricity to the engine in the engine room to your right." Suddenly, the lights switched off. Noah and Zeo turned on the flashlights in their phone and entered the engine room. They reached the main engine and Zeo connected the wires of the main engine with the wires of the main electric panel of the mansion. Suddenly, Jane got started again. She said "Sir, there is a secret base underneath. For going there, you need to go to the main computer, put your hand on it, tell your whole name and say 'to the underground base.'" They both did the same that Jane told them to do. They soon entered the place and saw an incubator in which a robot was unconscious. They too programed the computer to unlock the robot. They successfully programmed the whole computer and now they can unlock it but they didn't unlock that robot right now. Then they moved further and saw a weaponry. There was a variety of weapons hung on the wall. Then they moved further and saw a garage in which there were a lot of land transport vehicles. Jane said "Sir, your parents were superheroes." They both were shocked to hear it. They then moved* *further and saw a ton of incubators and saw suits of different types inside them. An incubator had a note on it. Noah read it and the note said "From your mom and dad, Noah this suit is for you and your team for the right time". Noah saw numbers written on the top of the incubators. The incubator with the note was incubator number 9 and there were a total of 9 incubators. He asked Jane "Jane, by the way, how do I acquire these suits?" Jane asked "Sir, which one do you want?" Noah said "I want suit number 9 for me and suit number 8 for Zeo. As we both are the superheroes now." Suddenly, the glasses of incubator numbers 8 and 9 opened and it came out. They took the suit and were going back when Jane said "Sir, take your weapons from the weaponry according to your suit." They went to the weaponry and Zeo got daggers, an AK-47 and a gun which helps them swing. Noah got an axe, a machine gun and the same swinging gun which Zeo got. Noah and Zeo wore it and it fitted them that perfectly that their six-pack abs were seen very easily. Then they wore the weapon belt over the suit and then Noah said, going back to the armory "Hey, Zeo, come back. We have to hide our identities. For that, we need a mask." They designed themselves a mask that covered their whole face. Soon, they heard the doorbell. Then they ran towards the door and opened it. It was the postman and the postman gave them a letter and went away.*

# Chapter 3: The Office

**The letter read**

> **"From Daniel Williams,**
>
> **Mr. Noah and Mr. Zeo, you people can join us from today onwards.**
>
> **Regards,**
>
> **Genentech headquarters, South San Francisco"**

*They both were very happy as finally they got a job. They went into the underground base, in the garage and chose the red bikes and raced off to the office and they met the C.E.O. and they got the job of the presentation directors. Everything was going on well until an enormous blimp came and some thieves came and barged in the nearby bank and were robbing it. Noah told Zeo about it. Zeo also looked at it. They ran to the C.E.O. and Zeo pretended like he was choked and Noah said "Sir, he is getting choked sir, can we go to the terrace for some fresh air?" Daniel agreed. Noah and Zeo ran. They went to the terrace and they took out their clothes and their superhero suit was present in there. Zeo and Noah took out their swinging guns and aimed at the blimp and they swung and stood over the airbus. Noah said "Okay, Zeo you have to barge in and take the airbus to the nearby lake and I will keep these people busy here." Zeo soon barged in and took the airbus to the water, and on the other side, Noah barged in the bank. He broke the glass and punched a big, fat guy in the jaw. There were total 5 thieves there. The big guy who was punched in the jaw ran towards Noah and they were having a fight. Soon, the fight ended and 4/5 people were finished up. The last and the strongest one was left. He was winning over Noah. The strongest person punched Noah in the face and then in the stomach which made Noah bled from the face and sent him to the window. The fifth guy was coming to punch him, but suddenly, the big guy turned back and it was Zeo with a wooden stick in his hand!!! Suddenly, he started running. The big guy followed him. Suddenly, there was no way to run away, then when the fifth guy was about to punch Zeo, Zeo's hand shot electricity, which sent the fifth guy to the wall and he got stunned. Zeo was also stunned. It was good that they had a mask which they wore which had hidden their identity till now. Noah handed the thieves to the police. He woke up Zeo and they returned on the terrace and wore their clothes and entered the office. The C.E.O. asked "Is Zeo fine now, Noah?" Noah says "Yes boss." They returned home soon and parked the bike in the garage underneath. They both returned at the night. And they then slept and woke up early in the morning.*

# <u>*Chapter 4: School Old Times*</u>

*Noah and Zeo reached and they saw that a letter was present in the letterbox. Noah read the letter loud "From your greatest villain, Me is at me base. If you people want to catch me, you can come at me base and catch me." Noah and Zeo got in the car and they wore their suit. Zeo started the car and it flew off the garage. Noah told Zeo the address which was under the East River. They parked the car and they dived inside the river and saw a main whole lid which they opened and saw a base. They went inside and they saw a big, black robot which started attacking them. Noah said "Jane, I need an axe." Jane told Noah and Zeo "Sir, there is a kind of laptop keyboard on your left arm. Now, you can press any button and the weapon you are thinking about will come in your hand." Zeo chose knuckles and Noah chose an axe. Noah ran first and separated one of the robot's hands but the robot regenerated it! Noah asked "Jane, what is this thing made up of?" Jane said "Sir, it is made up of 100% molten iron. You need to close it into containers after you break it into pieces." Noah told Zeo all this and said "You just have to do as I say." Noah told Zeo to get some get container from Jane. Zeo said "Jane, I need some containers." Some containers suddenly came in Zeo's hands. Noah also took some containers. Noah ran and separated the robot's right arm. Zeo ran and closed the right arm's liquid in the container. Zeo ran and separated the robot's left arm and Noah closed it in the container. One by one, the whole robot's liquid was closed. The robot then shut downed and a hologram projection came out of the robot. He saw the fire guy and they understood his plan, took the robot and put it in the car and then they flew to portfolio school of New York. After some time, they reached there. Then they saw that it was a huge zeppelin which was throwing a ray downwards which was making all the people float. Noah told Zeo to keep the people as safe as possible over here until he returns. Noah aims and shoots his swing gun at the zeppelin. He grabbed the zeppelin and placed a purple circle on the zeppelin which used lasers to make a hole big enough for Noah to fit inside. Noah entered into the zeppelin and saw that no one was there and a computer was there but it didn't contain anything. Suddenly, a rope came in Noah's neck and started suffocating him. It was the fire guy. Noah suddenly got the rope out of his neck and tied the fire guy in it. Then, he threw the fire guy on the zeppelin's control panel. Noah told Zeo "Zeo, this airbus is going to crash I have to jump". Noah jumped and he fell hard on the ground and he fainted. On the other hand, Zeo saw the zeppelin going towards East River. Zeo came and stood in front of it and as he blinked his eyes, the zeppelins were surrounded in water which held the airbus and then suddenly it crashed in the East River and the Brooklyn Bridge. Suddenly, a rope came which tied up the whole zeppelin and it got pulled backwards and two huge shurikens were thrown at the zeppelin and it busted as it was a balloon. After some time, Noah woke up and he was in the hospital. Noah woke up and he was in the hospital. He saw that he was damaged a lot and then Zeo came and then he said "Now we can go home." Noah agreed and then they reached the mansion. It was clean there and the dogs were sleeping. They came there and they had a nap. Noah dreamt that it was the fire guy who had killed his parents. He saw Lucas on the border of Russia fighting for America and then the fire guy with his companion came and burnt him because on the day when Lucas's dead body was brought, Noah saw that it was all burnt up!! And on the day when returned from the college, he saw someone who was putting Emma on fire, he thought that it was the fire guy who had burnt him.*

# <u>Chapter 5: The Darkness of Night</u>

*They returned and they also slept. The puppies woke up all of a sudden and they woke up Zeo and Noah. They all went out and saw Liam burning the house. Noah ran and punched Liam in the face. Liam kicked Noah in the face and then punched Zeo in the face. Then, Zeo and Noah fell down on the ground hard. The dogs started biting Liam but he took the dogs to the Sacramento River in order to drown them. As he was going to sink the dogs, suddenly he felt an immense energy level and a load of light behind him. Liam turned backed and left the dogs and saw a person who was glowing in a golden energy and then that person grabbed Liam from the jaw and threw him at the other side of the river. That person then flew and then he threw Liam on one of the poles of golden gate bridge which shook the bridge and road a little. Some stones fell in that person's hand. Liam asked "Who are you?" That person replied "I am Zeoh." He was a fusion of Zeo and Noah. Zeoh took a stone and bashed it in Liam's face. Zeoh then punched Liam which sent him flying to the other side of the river. Then, Zeoh punched him once again. Then, Liam stopped and went to attack Zeoh. Liam started punching Zeoh on the chest. After some time, Liam was very tired but there was not even a scratch on Zeoh's body. Zeoh smirked and punched Liam in the stomach which caused a huge explosion that broke the golden gate bridge completely. The next morning, Zeo and Noah woke up and saw the golden gate bridge which was totally broke down. Then, they took the dogs with them and they went back to the house. They took a bathe and then they had their breakfast. Noah, Zeo and the dogs will remember what had happened last night. After a week, they went to their offices and Daniel asked "How were your holidays, huh?" They said "Umm, yeah. They were good." Others people in the office asked "Hey, Noah, Zeo. How are you? Daniel told us that you were ill. Was it* true?" Noah and Zeo played dumb. They said "Umm, yeah, we were ill." They then started to work and they were waiting for their next mission but it looked like that the light of goodness had victory over the darkness of evil. They then returned home and they slept but they woke up all of a sudden and they went to the garage in order to upgrade the vehicles and they had upgraded their bike till now. Then, they started upgrading their vehicles and then it became boring. Zeo said "Hey, Noah, I want to go to the Disneyland right away." Suddenly, the alarm beeped. It means a mission has come out of somewhere. Finally, Noah and Zeo got a mission.

# Chapter 6: The Disney Adventures

*Noah then saw that the wristbands that they were wearing were beeping. Jane told them "Sir, Liam is in the jail." They were very happy after listening this Noah and Zeo asked Jane "Jane, what is the location of the mission?" Jane said "Sir, it is Disneyland." Noah asked "Who could it be at 8 pm in Disneyland? Is it a kid?" Jane said "No sir, it's Liam." Noah asked, getting annoyed "When will we get rid of this person?" Zeo shrugged his shoulders. Noah said "But, your wish is fulfilled." Zeo said "Yeah, but not in the way I wanted." Noah and Zeo sat on the bikes and raced to Disneyland. They saw a fire on the giant wheel and then they saw Liam setting fire on the other rides. There were other people also who were wearing a horrific mask and they were slaughtering the kids and the other people there. Suddenly, they activated their binoculars and they were just setting the plan when suddenly they saw a kid who flew upwards and then suddenly a green transparent shield and a blue sword came in his hand. Noah and Zeo were very surprised after seeing the little kid's superpowers. The people who were slaughtering others started shooting flames out of their flamethrower but the kid lowered his shield and then he went to the other people and pushed them backwards using the shield. But the shield and the sword of the kid were weird as they had a prehnite embedded in it. Noah and Zeo went for Liam. They grabbed Liam by his shoulders and threw him at the Giant wheel. The kid came towards Noah and Zeo. Suddenly, Liam came and he was about to attack the kid but the kid placed his shield and Zeo again grabbed Liam and threw him at the giant wheel again. Noah said "I wonder, how hungry is he for a punch?" That kid introduced himself to Noah and Zeo. His name was Prehnite, he was 10 years old. Noah and Zeo also introduced themselves and they thought of keeping Prehnite in their team. Noah took Prehnite on his bike and they raced back to their base. Zeo also sat on the bike and reached the base. Noah told Prehnite about the whole. Zeo asked "Noah, where will Prehnite sleep?" Noah said "Zeo, now you can sleep in my parents' bedroom and Prehnite can sleep with me." Prehnite requested Noah to keep his father over here too. Noah couldn't refuse. The next morning, they went for getting Prehnite's dad. Soon, they found him and then they took him to the base. Noah said "Prehnite, let's go and get your mom here." Prehnite said, sad "My mother is not in the world now?" Noah said "Oh, I understand." Prehnite's dad introduced himself. His name was Mark. Noah asked Mark "Why did you name your son Prehnite?" Mark replied "Because when he was born, he had a prehnite embedded in his chest." Mark also discussed about Prehnite's elder sister. Her name was Ruby Hessonite. Mark told alike Prehnite, Ruby also had some powers of fire and water. Mark told that soon she is going to come here from Australia today in an hour. She was there for her studies. Noah and Zeo went to airport for receiving ruby to their base. Soon, they reached and Zeo took out a huge board with "Ruby, we are here" on it. Soon, the people who were coming from Australia came out of the airport. A lady was coming towards them. Her eyes were as red as a ruby and her hair were as golden orange as a hessonite. Noah saw that she had a ruby embedded on her left arm and a hessonite embedded on her right arm. That lady came towards Noah and Zeo and asked them how do they know her? Noah told everything to that lady. That lady said "Oh, then you have met the right girl. I am Ruby Hessonite."*

# <u>Chapter 7: The Team Up</u>

*Noah and Zeo asked Ruby "Will you join our team?" Ruby said "Yes, of course." They took Ruby to their base. Prehnite came running towards Ruby and hugged her. Ruby caressed him and said "Hey, marshmallow, it has been a long time meeting you." Mark came there and saw Ruby there. He ran and hugged her also. Ruby said "Dad, it has been a long time meeting you too." Noah was going to make the dinner. Everybody was sitting on the dining table. Zeo turned his head towards Noah, who was cooking the dinner. Suddenly, the pan which contained hot but uncooked chicken was flipped and it was about to fall on the ground, but suddenly, Noah shot flame from his fingers which cooked the chicken and sent all the gravy and chicken back to the pan. Zeo said "How did you do that?" Noah shrugged. Noah soon served the dinner and after eating it, they all slept. Suddenly, the alarm beeped which meant that it was another mission for them. Noah and Zeo gave Prehnite and Ruby a suit and a mask that fitted them. Noah told Prehnite and Ruby to sit in the car. Noah drove it and asked Jane "Jane, where is our mission?" Jane said "Sir, it's a bank robbery. The bank is Access One Bank in Brooklyn." Noah said "Okay, so it's gonna take some time for us to reach it. Zeo activate boosts!" Zeo pulled a lever. The car turned into a jet and three turbines came out from the rear of the jet which gave them boost. Ruby and Prehnite were excited for their first mission. Soon, they reached the bank. Everybody walked out of the jet and went towards the bank. Noah saw 16 people there which meant that there were 8 thieves and 8 bank employees. Each thief had put a gun on each employee's head. Noah said "Okay, now masks on." They all wore their masks. Noah explained the plan. He suddenly broke the glass of the bank and he hid behind the wall. One of the thieves came near the broken glass. Noah grabbed the thief and took him. After some time, they all fainted the thief. Another thief said "Come out here!" Noah came and laughed and said "Hi there, I am Noah Marshal" The thieves aimed their guns on Noah's head. Noah said "Ok, cover!" Prehnite came there with the green, transparent shield which had a prehnite embedded in it and he said "Copy!" All thieves started shooting but all the bullets were stopped by the shield. Zeo came there and he called the authorities. A rope suddenly came in her hand. She ran and tied all of the thieves right away. Soon, the authorities were there and they arrested them. Noah told the police "They are all yours." They all sat in the jet and flew away. They all sat in the jet and they reached the base. Noah and all of them slept. They were all very tired. After the sun rose up high in the sky, they all woke up and decided to eat breakfast and go to the training room which was in the secret base. Zeo made avocado toast with egg. It's a healthy breakfast and now they all are superheroes now. The alarm suddenly beeped and they all had eaten their breakfast. Noah asked Jane "What is the location?" Jane said "Sir, the peaks of Kashmir." Noah asked "Do we have a jet?" Jane said "Yes sir." They all went into the garage and found a huge jet. Noah opened the gate of the garage and sat in the jet and they set out for the peaks of Kashmir.*

# Chapter 8: The India's Snow

Noah told the plan to everyone as they were piloting the jet. Noah asked Jane "Jane, what is Liam doing there?" Jane said "Sir, he is trying to melt all the ice and snow." Zeo said "According to my calculations, Kashmir's whole ice and snow if gets converted into water, will be enough to flood the whole India!" Noah started explaining the plan. He said "Zeo, you and I will jump to the mountains straight on Liam using our wingsuits that I have inserted in your suit and we also have a chute inside our suit. It will open on our voice command. Then Prehnite, you and Ruby will come downwards and Ruby you will stop Liam using your water powers; Prehnite, now you will defend us all using your shield and then you will get upwards back to the jet using this gun." Noah gave Prehnite the swing gun and continued "And on my signal, you have to throw this rope." Noah brought a rope and tied it to a nail which was inserted in the floor of the jet. Zeo said "Noah, we have reached." Noah told Zeo to activate his wingsuit. Noah saw that it was all foggy right there. They deployed their wingsuit and Noah slid a part of the floor of the jet and they found Liam under there jet. Noah and Zeo jumped and fell over Liam. But it was a hologram of Liam. Suddenly, Noah pointed at the jet. Zeo asked Noah "What is it?" Zeo turned around and saw what Noah wanted him to see. They saw that Liam was standing on the jet. Liam jumped and he threw fire at the jet which sent the jet backwards towards a huge mountain. Zeo shot his swing gun towards the jet and he was slipping down the peak. He saw a tree and he grabbed it. Noah also came and helped Zeo. The tree suddenly broke down. Zeo yelled as he turned golden and however fused with Noah "Graaaaaaah!" Zeoh flew towards the jet and grabbed it. The jet stopped from collapsing from the mountain. Then, he saw Liam who overturned and saw Zeoh and he remembered what had happened last time with him when Noah and Zeo had fused into Zeoh and he was running away. Zeoh said "Back up down here." Ruby *and Prehnite jumped using their wingsuits and ruby threw water on Liam. Liam was falling when Zeoh caught Liam and suddenly Liam threw fire on Zeoh when suddenly a green shield came in between and deflected the fire. It was Prehnite's shield. Liam got hit by his own fire. Zeoh threw Liam towards ruby. Suddenly, Ruby's fists grew bigger!! Ruby punched Liam in the head which broke the mountain and Liam went deeper in the earth. Suddenly, Ruby stood in front of him and punched him in the face and which sent Liam flying upwards in the sky. Zeoh was waiting for Liam to go flying upwards. As he saw Liam rising upwards in the sky, he flew towards him and he hit his hands on Liam's back after which he fell on the ground and a white colored, snowy and cold fog. Zeoh came down. Zeo and Noah separated and Noah told everybody to get back to the jet. Noah climbed and grabbed the floor of the jet, and as soon they reached America, Noah got Liam arrested. As they all reached home, they saw that the dogs were spreading dirt in the whole house. After cleaning, Noah switched on the T.V. and saw a news.*

# <u>*Chapter 9: The Launch Dates*</u>

*They turned on the T.V. and a shocking news flashed on the T.V. It said "A group of asteroids is going to crash with our Earth on 11<sup>th</sup> July 2018. That means 3 months later. If it collides with the Earth, our planet will get converted into space dust!!" Noah said "Zeo, get ready with the car outside. We have to go to the prison." Zeo said "What?" Noah said "Get in the car. We are leaving for the prison." Zeo and Noah left for the prison and soon reached there. Noah asked inspector Sam Anderson "Can we talk to Liam?" Sam said "Okay but be careful. His superpowers are still with him." Noah and Zeo went inside and told Liam about how* Earth's *gonna get destroyed but it looked like Liam don't want to save the* Earth. *After loads of Noah's requests, Liam agreed with Noah. Then, they went to the base and they decided of building a rocket that would contain guns and missile launchers. Then, first Zeo brought the materials that will be used for building and Liam and Noah were building a rocket. After 2 months, their hard work resulted fruitfully. They made a huge rocket that contained three pods enough for Noah, Zeo and Liam to fit in and control it. It also had boosters, missile launchers and guns attached to it. Now, Noah, Zeo and Liam were waiting for 9<sup>th</sup> July 2018 and it was the date finalized for the rocket launch. Noah was still not believing in Liam as he has done a ton of crimes. Noah went to the rocket in the night when everybody slept. He added a button on his pod which he connected to Zeo's, Ruby's and Prehnite's pod and he named it "eject." He then went and slept. Noah had a plan ready if Liam betrays them. Noah had thought that if Liam betrays them, Noah will press the button which he had attached to the other people's room which will eject all of the pods. Suddenly, he heard a voice. As Noah sneaked to the place which made the sound, he saw Liam. He was searching for something. He first took out a screwdriver and threw it away. Then, he took a wrench and threw it away. Then, he took out a hammer and* *threw it away. Then, he took a knife and nodded and put it in the pant pocket. He then searched for more things, but luckily, Noah had identified Liam's intention of searching these types of things. He understood that all of a sudden, he will hit him with the knife that he has. Noah saw Liam finding more things. He saw that Liam took out a gun and saw that it didn't have any ammos so he started searching for ammos and soon he found it. Then, he filled the gun with the ammos. Noah then sneaked back to his room and slept. Well, Noah knew that Liam would be doing something like this.*

# <u>*Chapter 10: 3 … 2 … 1 … Launch!!!*</u>

*Then, on 9th July, they woke up and they entered the rocket. Liam said "Space oxygen deploying on." Zeo said "Guns and launchers activated." Noah said "Boosts ON." Ruby said "Jane inserting done." Prehnite said "Rocket ready for launch." They said together "3 … 2 … 1 … Launch!!" The rocket was launched and it flew in the air, cutting through the air, they were out of the Earth's atmosphere and they soon saw the group of asteroids. Noah told Zeo to start shooting missiles and bullets on the asteroids as Zeo was in charge of shooting. Soon, the asteroids were turned into ashes now. Noah told Liam "Liam, now, take us back." But there was no response from the other side. Noah started shouting "Liam, Liam!!! Liam!!!" Then, Noah suddenly felt something hard on his head. As he turned around, he saw Liam behind him who was holding a knife in his hand which had Noah's blood on it. Then, Noah was unconscious. After 2 hours of unconsciousness, Noah finally woke up and had recalled everything that happened to him before his unconsciousness. Noah searched the whole rocket for Liam but except Zeo no one was there. Noah pressed an eject button which was present in Noah's room. After some time, the whole ship was ejected but Zeo, Ruby and Prehnite didn't have any information about what had happened to Noah and he thought "I think Noah wants to send me back to Earth." Zeo said "Jane, get back to Earth." Zeo's pod deployed boosters which helped him a lot in reaching the Earth. On the other hand, Noah said "Jane, track Liam!" The scanning started and was successful. Noah found Liam but he was far from Noah. Noah told Jane "Jane, deploy my suit." Noah's suit was there. Noah opened the pod and flew towards Liam who was going back to Earth. Noah ordered Jane "Jane, deploy boosters." The suit's boosters were deployed. Noah's speed was 5 times faster now. After he was a lot near Liam, he came in front of Liam and punched* him in the chest and face. Liam was pushed back a lot. Noah flew towards Liam and punched him once again. Liam was once again sent back. Noah once again came towards Liam and kicked him. Liam was once again pushed back. Liam suddenly stopped and when Noah came, he was grabbed by his legs and then Liam threw him to the moon. Noah crashed on the moon and then Noah and Liam stood on the moon. Then, they fought with each other. On the other hand, Zeo and the others landed on Earth successfully and saw two shadows fighting with each other on the moon as it was 9:00 pm on Earth.

# Chapter 11: The Fight

On the other hand, Noah grabbed Liam after which he said "Noah, please leave me! Please forgive me! Will you not forgive your own big brother?" Noah said "I don't have a brother." Liam said "You have. I am yours." Noah fell for it. Suddenly, Liam hit his elbow on Noah's face. Noah had started bleeding but still he punched Liam in the face repeatedly. Noah threw Liam away from the moon and he crashed into the Venus. Noah grabbed a moonstone and went near Liam. Noah bashed the moonstone on Liam's head until Liam's face bled and the stone was turned into powder. Liam grabbed Noah and threw him on the planet Mars. They both stood on it. Noah said as he took his fighting stance "Hey, enough of this warm-up, now let's start the real fight." Liam and Noah ran towards each other and Noah flipped and placed something on Liam's back. Noah jumped backwards saying "Boom." The weird square that Noah had attached on Liam's back exploded but still Liam didn't even have a scratch on his body!! Noah was surprised. Suddenly, Liam flew towards Noah and he punched Noah in the stomach which sent Noah flying and he crashed in the mountains present on Mars. Noah's whole face was drenched with his blood. Soon, Liam punched on Noah's neck which choked him. Liam grabbed Noah's neck and started knocking him against the floor. Liam stopped knocking Noah and asked him "Any last word?" Noah said "Oh, yes. I forgot to tell you that there is a crap attached right behind your neck." As Liam turned around, he saw a grenade and a flash bang attached on his back. As he turned to Noah, he saw that Noah wasn't there. Suddenly, the grenade and the flash bang exploded and blinded Liam and sent him flying into a volcano. Noah was going to fly when suddenly, he stopped as he heard a roar. As Noah turned around and saw Liam who was now a lava monster who grabbed Noah. Liam was squeezing Noah in order to kill him. Noah *suddenly threw a flash bang in Liam's eyes. The flash bang exploded and blinded Liam and forced him to leave Noah. Noah fell and suddenly turned golden. Noah crouched and he was generating energy for a huge soul bomb. Soon, Liam's blindness was over and he said as he was searching for Noah "Where are you, Noah? I can sense your presence." Suddenly, he saw Noah whose shirt was completely ripped. He was about to release the soul bomb but Liam kicked Noah in the face and crunched Noah's right leg. Liam was about to crunch Noah when suddenly, Noah shot fire in one of Liam's eyes. Liam said "How dare you? How dare you damage my face?" Liam grabbed and started squeezing Noah "I'll squeeze the life out of you and then rip you in half." Noah suddenly felt an energy and Noah released the energy, and luckily, it was the soul bomb that sent Liam flying away and he fell head first. Liam who was right then a monster turned into a normal human who had fire superpowers. Liam stood up and tried to leave but he wasn't able to do it as Noah had grabbed him. Noah said as he attached a booster on his back and turned it on "So too quick Mr. Liam!" Liam flew away and Noah set out for Earth. He first sat in the pod and went into the atmosphere of Earth.*

# ***Epilogue***

*As Noah entered the Earth's atmosphere, the pod broke down. Noah then deployed a chute but it tore. Then he deployed a wingsuit which helped Noah a lot to glide but it also got tore. Noah then was burning as he was falling. He was shining like a shooting star. On the other hand, Zeo and the others were standing outside, waiting for Noah to come when he saw a shooting star. He wished "I wish that Noah returns safely." As the shooting star crashed near him, he saw that it was Noah only!! Zeo said "Oh, my wish is fulfilled!" He took Noah to the hospital. Mr. Walter said "His right leg is all fractured. Thanks to God that his bones aren't broken and he is still alive but his energy is all drained and he has lost a lot of blood." Zeo said "Okay, you can take my blood." Zeo's blood was passed to Noah and then he was conscious. Noah was treated well and then he was strong and healthy. Zeo was very happy for Noah and then they left for home and Noah told Zeo everything that happened with him in the space. On the other hand, Liam crashed onto a planet far, far, far "ok not that far" but still it was far. Somebody came and supported him in standing up. Liam asked "Who are you? And what is this place?" The man said "I am God Hydro. And this is the planet Ash. I live here and it's far away from the solar system." Liam said "You look like a bad person." God Hydro said "Yeah, I have a motive, an evil motive to become immortal using the 14 containers. There are 14 of them on 14 different planets. Want to become my assistant? Well, I already have someone with me. His name is Stephen Hickens but still I can keep you with us also. Then, we all will become immortal." Liam said "Is Stephen Hickens our partner? Man, he had helped me murder Lucas Marshal or my father. As I had advised him to give me the blue liquid and we both will become immortal but still he refused and kicked me out of my house and then they changed their country." God Hydro said "Okay, that means we know each other very well. So, you're in?" Liam said "Yes, of course." God Hydro said "Okay, so let's first go for Shieldax." They all were wondering how will they reach there when suddenly Liam told them about his pod of the rocket.*

# The End

www.ingramcontent.com/pod-product-compliance
Lightning Source LLC
LaVergne TN
LVHW041129180726
843490LV00003B/1255